LITTLE MISS TROUBLE

by Roger Hargreaves

To Mummy

I may be trouble
im not this bad &
maybe you should buy me a Mr Small
it could be safer for you!!

Love
Annabel xx

EGMONT

"Here comes trouble," people used to say.

And who do you think would come walking along?

That's right!

Little Miss Trouble.

Oh, the trouble she caused.

One morning she went to see Mr Uppity.

"Do you know what Mr Small calls you behind your back?" she asked him.

"No," replied Mr Uppity. "What does Mr Small call me behind my back?"

Little Miss Trouble looked at him.

"Fatty!" she said.

Now, Mr Uppity didn't like that.

Not at all.

Not one little bit.

He went round immediately to see Mr Small.

"How dare you call me 'FATTY'?" he shouted.

"But ..." stammered Mr Small, who had never called him "Fatty".

"But ..."

"But nothing," shouted Mr Uppity.

And he hit poor Mr Small.

Ouch!

And gave him a black eye.

Poor Mr Small.

Little Miss Trouble, who was hiding behind a tree, hugged herself with glee.

"Oh, I do so like making trouble," she giggled to herself.

Naughty girl!

Little Miss Trouble went to see Mr Clever.

"Do you know what Mr Small calls you behind your back?" she asked him.

"No," replied Mr Clever. "Tell me! What does Mr Small call me behind my back?"

Little Miss Trouble looked at him.

"Big Nose!" she said.

Now.

Mr Clever didn't like that very much either.

Off he rushed.

And, when he found Mr Small, without waiting for an explanation, he punched him!

Hard!

In the other eye!

Poor Mr Small.

Two black eyes for something he'd never done.

"Oh, look at you," Miss Trouble laughed when she saw him.

"It's all your fault," said Mr Small.

"True," she said.

And walked off.

Poor Mr Small had to go to the doctor.

"Good heavens!" exclaimed Doctor Makeyouwell when he saw him. "Whatever happened to you?"

Mr Small explained.

"I think," Doctor Makeyouwell said when he'd heard what Mr Small had to tell him, "that something should be done about that little lady! What she needs is …"

Then he stopped.

And he chuckled.

"That's it," he laughed.

"What's it?" asked Mr Small.

And Doctor Makeyouwell whispered something to Mr Small.

Would you like to know what he whispered?

Not telling you!

It's a secret!

That afternoon Mr Small went to see Mr Tickle.

"Do you know what Miss Trouble calls you behind your back?" he asked.

"No," said Mr Tickle. "What does Miss Trouble call me behind my back?"

Mr Small looked at him.

"Pudding Face!" he said.

Then Mr Small went to see Mr Bump.

"Do you know what Miss Trouble calls you behind your back?" he asked.

"No," said Mr Bump. "What does Miss Trouble call me behind my back?"

Mr Small looked at him.

"Mr Nitwit!" he said.

Little Miss Trouble was in trouble.

"How dare you call me 'Pudding Face'?" cried Mr Tickle.

And tickled her.

"And how dare you call me 'Mr Nitwit'?" cried Mr Bump.

And bumped her.

Now, I don't know whether you've ever been tickled and bumped at the same time, but it's not much fun. In fact, it's no fun at all.

Ticklebumpticklebumpticklebumpticklebump!

For ten minutes. And ten minutes of ticklebumping is a long time. I can tell you!

Later that evening Doctor Makeyouwell strolled round to see Mr Small.

"How are the eyes?" he asked.

"Oh, much better now, thank you," replied Mr Small.

"And did our little plan work?" asked the doctor.

"It did indeed," grinned Mr Small.

"Shake," said Doctor Makeyouwell.

And they shook hands.

Well.

Not quite hands.

Doctor Makeyouwell then strolled round to see Miss Trouble.

She was feeling very sorry for herself.

"What's wrong with you?" he asked her.

And she told him all about it.

All about everything.

Doctor Makeyouwell looked at her.

"Cheer up," he said.

"You know what you've just had, don't you?"

Little Miss Trouble shook her head.

"A taste of your own medicine!" he chuckled.

And went home.

For supper.

EARLY READER

Beast Quest

Arax
the Soul Stealer

Arax the Soul Stealer was originally published
as a Beast Quest special. This version has been
specially adapted for developing readers.

*You will earn one special gold coin for every chapter
you finish. Find out what to do with your coins at
the back of the book!*

1

With special thanks to Jan Burchett, Sara
Vogler and Fiona Munro

Reading Consultant: Prue Goodwin, lecturer in literacy and
children's books

ORCHARD BOOKS
Carmelite House
50 Victoria Embankment
London EC4Y 0DZ

Arax the Soul Stealer first published in 2009
This Early Reader edition published in 2015
Text © Beast Quest Limited 2009, 2015
Cover and inside illustrations by Steve Sims © Beast Quest Limited 2009, 2015

ISBN 978 1 40833 922 0

Printed in China

Orchard Books
An imprint of Hachette Children's Group
Part of The Watts Publishing Group Limited
An Hachette UK Company

www.hachette.co.uk
www.beastquest.co.uk